Elizabeth Prentiss

Little Susy's Six Teachers

SALZWASSER
VERLAG

Elizabeth Prentiss

Little Susy's Six Teachers

Reprint of the original, first published in 1864.

1st Edition 2022 | ISBN: 978-3-75259-421-8

Verlag (Publisher): Salzwasser Verlag GmbH, Zeilweg 44, 60439 Frankfurt, Deutschland
Vertretungsberechtigt (Authorized to represent): E. Roepke, Zeilweg 44, 60439 Frankfurt, Deutschland
Druck (Print): Books on Demand GmbH, In de Tarpen 42, 22848 Norderstedt, Deutschland

LITTLE SUSY'S

SIX TEACHERS.

BY HER

AUNT SUSAN.

NEW-YORK:

1864.

"So Mrs. Love took her to her mamma."—P. 12, 2d Series.

Teachers.

LITTLE SUSY'S SIX TEACHERS.

CHAPTER I.

PERHAPS you think you are going to hear that Little Susy went to school. But you are not. All the teachers she had, lived in the house with her. And all the lessons they taught her, were lessons without books. I shall not tell you even the names of half of them, lest you should get tired. I shall tell you of only six.

It is a common saying that, "Babies bring love into the world with them." If you ask your mamma whether you did, I know what she will say. She will smile kindly upon you, and say: "Yes, indeed, you little dear." So Susy brought her first teacher with her, and her name was Mrs. Love. She was just such a teacher as a baby likes. She had a gentle, sweet face, and a soft, kind voice; her cheeks were of a beautiful rose-color, and her forehead was smooth and white. Most of the other teachers consulted her before they taught Susy any lessons; and Mr. Pain, who was one of them, often staid away weeks at a time because Mrs. Love took such good care of Susy herself. Mr. Pain was not so pleasant to look at, as Mrs. Love. He looked rather pale and tired. He was grave and serious, and his forehead was wrinkled. But for all that, he taught Susy some very good lessons, and even Mrs. Love sometimes sent for him.

Did you ever see a little lamb bounding over the soft grass? Did you ever hear a bird sing to another bird away out in the woods?

If you ever did, you know how Miss Joy looked when she came

dancing in to see Susy, and how her voice sounded when she taught her such pleasant lessons as she knew how to teach. She was a little bit of a creature, with waving, sunny hair, and bright eyes, sparkling with health and happiness. I believe she and Mrs. Love are sisters. At any rate they look more or less alike.

Susy's third teacher had several names. His easiest name was Mr. Ought. He did not look much like Miss Joy. Susy did not like him at first. He was so tall, and taught her such hard lessons, and when she would not listen, so often called Mr. Pain to come and punish her, that she wished he would go away and never come back. But the more she looked at him the more kind and dear his face appeared, and by and by she learned to love him with all her heart.

The fifth teacher was Aunt

Patience. She looked as if she had seen a good deal of trouble. But you must not fancy she looked sad, or sour, or bitter, or any thing bad or disagreeable. There was a serene smile on her face that made you love her at once.

Another beautiful and holy teacher lived with Susy. His name was Faith. He was not older than Susy herself, and the only reason he knew any more than she did, was this. He was an Angel. He knew a good deal about heaven, and about Jesus. He could tell her sweet stories from the Bible. His eyes shone just as stars shine in the sky, and his face looked peaceful, like the face of Aunt Patience, but more radiant and cheerful. Susy liked him, and he liked her.

Have you so many teachers in your house? Perhaps you say, No. But I am sure you have, and if you read on perhaps you will see. To be sure, your Mrs. Love may not be exactly like Susy's Mrs. Love. But in most things she is.

CHAPTER II.

When Susy was born, Mrs. Love came with her, as I have told you. She took the little baby gently in her arms, and smiled upon her tenderly. If she had left her lying there, Susy would have died; and then I could not have written this book.

Then Mrs. Love dressed her in soft, warm clothes. She put on a little tiny shirt, a flannel petticoat, a white frock, and such wee morsels of socks that when Susy grew up she gave them to her doll. I don't know whether you had on any socks, or not. Perhaps your Mrs. Love said your little feet ought to keep each other warm, and mustn't wear socks.

It took some time to dress Susy. She was so small and weak that she could not help dress herself, nor hold up her head. But there was one thing she knew how to do, that no body ever taught her. She knew how to double up her little mite of a hand and suck it as hard as she could. I suppose she thought she was hungry.

Do you suppose she would be alive now if she had had nothing but her hand to eat? No, indeed! So Mrs. Love took her to her mamma, who was very glad to give her some nice, warm breakfast. If Mrs. Love had not been there, I dare say her mamma would not have given her any. Very likely she would have said: "Oh! don't bring that child here! I'm tired, and want to go to sleep!" But then you know Mrs. Love was there!

Now what do you think little Susy's first lesson was? Why, she had to learn to smile!

Mrs. Love kept smiling and smiling, till at last Susy began to think to herself that perhaps she could do so too. So she really smiled. Then you should have seen and heard what went on.

"I declare! this child has just smiled," said her nurse.

"Oh! are you sure?" cried her mamma. "Bring her to me; let me see!"

"Little darling!" said Mrs. Love.

When her papa came home to dinner that day, the nurse met

him in the hall, and said to him: "The baby has smiled!"

And when he went up to the nursery, Mrs. Love said: "Baby has learned to smile!"

And when he asked Susy's mamma how she did, she only said in a joyful voice: "Don't you think, our baby has smiled!"

So by that time he smiled, though he shook his head, as much as to say: "I don't believe it!"

After this Mrs. Love made every body in the house hug and kiss Susy so much, that it was a wonder how the little thing found room to grow. They did not kiss her on purpose, you know, but because they could not help it. Every thing she did delighted the whole family, and one day the cook said:

"I do believe this child is going to have a dent in her chin; and if she has a dent in her chin, I shall give up !"

She meant by that, that she liked dents in people's chins.

It was not long after this that Mrs. Love taught Susy to put up her little hand and pat her mamma's chin and cheek ; and then to give her sweet kisses ; and then to wind her fat, soft arms around her neck. And Miss Joy was almost always teaching her to spring and dance, and to be such

2

a happy little baby, that it was a pleasure to go into the nursery and hear her shout, and laugh, and clap her hands, and see her face all full of smiles.

CHAPTER III.

BUT when Susy began to run about, and could reach up to the table where her mamma's work-basket stood, some body besides kind Mrs. Love and laughing Miss Joy, had to come and teach her. For there were scissors in the basket, and pins and needles, and Susy made up her mind that she would play with them. Everyday, when she put up her hand to take the basket, her mamma would shake her head, and say: "No, no!" And Susy would then begin to cry, and after a minute or two, would snatch the basket again. One day, her mamma was talking with another lady, and she did not see Susy when she put her hand out towards her basket. So Susy took it, and sat down upon the floor to have a good time with it. She tangled all the spools of thread together, and unrolled all the tape. She threw the buttons all over the floor. She took a piece of ribbon that her mamma had bought to tie her little shirts with, and put it round her neck. She tossed the hooks and eyes into a corner, and let a ball of yarn roll under the table. For all this time she was trying to get at the needle-book, which lay at the bottom of the basket. Just as she reached it, her mamma looked down, and said: "No, no!" Susy knew very well what that meant, but she held on to the needle-book until all of a sudden Mr. Pain gave her such a prick that she let it drop. He had scratched her with one of the needles. Susy gave a scream, and looked very angrily at the needle-book, which she had now learned not to touch. But it was only a few days after this, that she went to the fire-place and filled her clean white apron with coals and ashes. Her mamma took them away from her, and shook her head, and said: "No, no!" again and again. But as soon as Susy had another clean apron put on, she ran again to the fire and began to fill it with coals, and no matter how often her mamma said, No, no! she would keep doing it, over and over. Then Mrs. Love said to her mamma: "If we let Susy do so, some day she will get burned. We ought to punish her, so that she will mind when she is spoken to." "Yes, I think so, too," said her mamma.

So Mrs. Love called Mr. Pain, and told him to slap Susy's little arms if she disobeyed again. It was not long before he had to come; and as soon as she saw him, Miss Joy, who had been frolicking with Susy a whole year, and never before had been absent from her—poor Miss Joy ran away and hid. As soon as Susy felt the slaps on her arm, she let the coals drop, and began to cry. She looked at her arm, which bore the red marks of Mr. Pain's hand, and pitied it very much. But the slap did her good. It taught her to obey her mamma about the fire, and saved her from being burned up, as she certainly would have been if she had kept on playing with the coals.

Mr. Pain soon went away, and

he had hardly turned his back, when Miss Joy peeped out of the closet where she had been hiding, and made such a funny little face that Susy could not help laughing, and her face was both wet with tears and shining with smiles. She kissed her mamma, and put her arms around her neck, and her mamma kissed her and said: "Susy won't be naughty any more." And Susy smiled, and said: "No, no!"

CHAPTER IV.

BEFORE Susy was old enough to understand what Mr. Ought said to her, he used to tell her mamma what she should do for her baby, and she would mind him directly. But as soon as Susy was able to listen, herself, to what he said, he came and lived in the nursery, and when she went to walk, he went with her, and when she played, he was near her. He never went to sleep, but was always wide awake; and you could not touch him with your little finger, no matter how softly, but he would start up to see what you meant.

One day when Susy was tired of playing with her toys, she began to look about the room for something new. There was an inkstand on the table, and she thought she would stand on tiptoe, and get it. But her mamma saw what she was doing, and she said: "No, Susy, no! you must not touch my inkstand."

Susy stopped a moment.

"Don't touch it," said Mr. Ought.

"I want it," said Susy. "I want it vely much." She put her hand upon it again, and looked at her mamma to see what she would do. But her mamma could not do any thing. She was lying sick in bed.

"Is my little Susy going to mind me?" said she.

Susy looked down, and did not answer. But her little fingers were on the inkstand.

"Oh! don't be naughty, Susy," said Mr. Ought.

Then Susy looked up, and smiled, and ran away from the table. She felt very happy because she had been obedient. Miss Joy took hold of her hands and began to dance, and Mrs. Love kissed her, and said: "Dear Susy! precious little Susy!" a good many times.

Do you know who was lying in the bed with her mamma? It was Robbie. Susy's little baby-brother. Two or three days after that, Susy did not feel well, and she thought she should like to sit in her mamma's lap and hear her sing. But there was Robbie lying upon it, taking up all the room. So she went up to him and pulled him by the frock, and said: "Get down, boy."

"He can't get down," said her mamma. "He is too little."

Then Susy was angry and she said to Robbie: "Go away, boy. Let Susy come up." And she lifted her hand, and was just going to strike her little brother. But just then, Mr. Ought said in quite a stern voice: "*Susy!*"

Then Susy stopped and listened. Her angry, red face began to grow pleasant; she sat down on the rug at her mamma's feet, and did not say another word. She had some teeth coming, and they made her feel almost sick, and always before this, if she did not feel well, she could sit in her mamma's lap and find comfort.

While she was sitting on the floor, her mamma felt sorry for her, and longed to take her in her arms, and kiss and soothe her. But now dear, good old Aunt

Patience came and sat down on the rug by Susy's side, and she took her little tired head right into her own kind bosom, wiped away all the tears, and said: "Never mind! By and by Robbie will go to sleep, and then it will be Susy's turn."

And Susy looked up into her mamma's anxious face, and said in a soft, sweet voice: "Never mind, mamma!"

CHAPTER V.

WHEN Susy went to bed, at night, her mamma, and Mrs. Love, and the little angel, Faith, always went with her. Her mamma would kneel down with her, and Susy would fold her hands, and pray to God to take care of her. And after she was in bed, and the clothes were nicely tucked about her, Mrs. Love would kiss her, and then they would go down stairs, leaving her all alone with Faith. Sometimes Susy would fall asleep as soon as her head touched her pillow, and sometimes she would lie awake, thinking. One night, when she was about three years old, she awoke from a sound sleep, and felt very lonely. The room was dark and still, and she had a great mind to begin to scream and cry. But just as she was opening her mouth, Mr. Ought said to her: "I wouldn't scream, if I were you. It frightens your mamma, and you know she isn't very well."

Then Susy only sat up in bed, and looked about, to see if her mamma were really not there.

"What's the matter, Susy?" asked Faith, coming very near her, and sitting down by her crib.

"I'm afraid of the dark," said Susy.

"Oh! I wouldn't be afraid," said

Faith. "God can see right through the dark, and He can see you. He won't let any thing hurt you."

"How do you know?"

"I know, because you asked Him to take care of you just before you went to sleep."

"Do you think he heard me when I arksed him?"

"Oh! yes. He can hear just as easy!"

Susy lay down, and was silent

a little while. But she still felt afraid. So she folded her hands together, and said softly: "O God! I am afraid of the dark. Please don't let it hurt me. I arks to you to take care of me. I arks to you to keep awake and take care of me. My mamma is not better enough to keep awake. Amen." Then Faith said: "I am sure God heard you. He will certainly take good care of you."

So Susy began to leave off feeling afraid. She put her hand under her cheek, shut her eyes, and fell into a sweet sleep. When her mamma came up to bed, she stopped in the nursery to look at Susy, and she saw a sweet, peaceful smile on her face.

"I wonder what she is dreaming about?" thought she.

In the morning Robbie crept into her bed, and kissed her till she awoke.

"Oh! is that you, Robbie?" said she. "Nursey! Robbie creep-ed right over you into my crib. Isn't he a little dear? I couldn't get to sleep last night, and I couldn't, and I couldn't. And at last God came and got me to sleep."

"O Susy!" said nurse.

"Well! I *thinked* He came," said Susy.

CHAPTER VI.

It was Christmas-day, and very cold. Susy and Miss Joy ran out of doors and threw snow at each other till their cheeks were like roses. Robbie sat in his high-chair at the nursery-window, and Susy threw little bits of snow up to him, and he kept trying to catch them. When Susy went in, she found Mrs. Love packing up baskets of good things to be sent away. There was one, not very large, but pretty heavy, full of sugar and tea for poor old Mrs. Hadn't Any.

"O mamma!" said Susy, "I can lift this basket! I can carry it four miles!"

Her mamma laughed.

"Well, I can carry it three miles," said Susy.

Her mamma only smiled, and kept on helping Mrs. Love fill the other baskets.

"I could carry it as far as across the street," said Susy.

"Yes, I suppose you could. And I do not know but I shall let you carry it," said Mrs. Love.

"All myself?"

"Yes, all yourself."

Then Susy was delighted indeed. She ran up stairs to get her coat and hood, and while nurse was putting them on, she said:

"Oh! I'm going to carry a great,

Susy and her Nurse.—P. 44, 1st Series.

Teachers.

big basket full of good things, to a poor woman!"

"I too!" said Robbie.

"Oh! no Robbie! you are not old enough. When you are as old as I am, then you shall go."

"Oh! I suppose you lived in the ark," said their nurse, patting her fat cheek.

Then Susy ran down stairs, and they put the basket in her hands, and told her to go straight across the street, and round the corner, and the very first house would be Mrs. Hadn't Any's.

Susy had never been out alone in her life. She took up the basket, and marched off, while they all watched her from the basement windows. The basket was heavy, but she did not mind that, because Miss Joy went with her and helped carry it. And then old Mrs. Hadn't Any was waiting at the door, all ready to take it, for she knew it was coming, and she wished Susy a "Merry Christmas!" and said: "Now I mean to have a nice, hot cup of tea for my Christmas!"

When Susy got home, Miss Joy could hardly let her stand still long enough to have her things taken off.

"O mamma!" said she: "it's nice to carry baskets to poor old women. It's better than hanging up stockings!"

"Indeed it is," said her mamma. "A great deal better. And I am going to send Robbie now to Mrs. Thankful's with ever so many things."

"Robbie is too little," said Susy.

"Don't be selfish, Susy," said Mr. Ought. Susy blushed.

"He is too little," said she. "He never walked out in his life."

"Oh! no, he isn't too little," said Mrs. Love. He carries the

Bible to his papa every morning, at prayers, and he never is so happy as when he has something to give away. He is a sweet child! Just as sweet as a lamb!"

"So he is!" said Susy. "I'm glad he is going. He shall wear my mittens if he wants to. And I'll look out of the window, and see him go."

Then Mr. Ought smiled on Susy with such a smile that she really felt as if the sun had been shining down to warm her.

"I begin to like Mr. Ought," thought she. "He is very pleasant."

"On the whole, Susy you may go with Robbie," said Mrs. Love. "You and Nurse can carry the basket, till you get to the house, and then you can give it to him."

So Susy and Miss Joy scampered up stairs, and they told Robbie all about it, and Robbie put his arms round Susy's neck and kissed her. And when he gave the basket to Mrs. Thankful, his face had more than a basket full of delight in it, and Susy was the very happiest little girl you ever saw.

CHAPTER VII.

You may think that after this, Susy did not wait for Mr. Ought to speak twice, but would mind his softest whisper. But the very next day, as she and Robbie were playing together, and Miss Joy was helping them build a house, a very sad affair happened, about which I will tell you. Robbie was a little bit of a rogue, and he liked to tease, as most boys do. He would come behind Susy and kiss her neck, and then run off and hide behind his nurse, who sat there at work. Then Susy would pretend to be quite angry, and would throw a block after him, and make believe cry. Then Robbie would creep out, softly, and kiss her again, or perhaps throw the block back at Susy. Now as Susy was two years older than Robbie, she could throw the block in such a way as not to hit him ; but Robbie could not throw so well, and pretty soon he threw a large block right into her face. The moment she felt it, Susy flew into a great rage, and caught up the first thing that she could find, to throw at Robbie, who was so frightened that he could not speak or move.

"Stop! stop!" said Mr. Ought. "Don't hurt your dear little brother. He was only playing."

"I won't stop!" said Susy. "He is a naughty, wicked boy. He hurted me on purpose!"

"Do you know that God is looking right at your little, angry face?" said Mr. Ought.

"I don't care!" said Susy, and was just going to throw at Robbie a great heavy wooden ball that she had snatched up in her anger, when she felt her hand seized from behind. She looked up, and saw her mamma's grieved face.

"Go into the closet," said Mr. Ought. "Go, before your mamma has to bid you. You are not fit to stay here."

Then Susy got up, sorrowfully, and went into the closet and shut the door. No dear Mrs. Love, no laughing Miss Joy went with her. She felt as if her heart would break.

"Oh! what a naughty little girl you are!" said Mr. Ought. "Do you think God loved you when you were so angry? Do you think the dear, holy children up in heaven do so?"

"No!" said Susy. "I don't think God loves me. I am very naughty. I will ask him to forgive me." Then she knelt down and clasped her hands and said: "O God! you are a good God. I love you, good God. I am sorry I was naughty. I hope you won't say I can't come in to heaven I want to come in, really." Her mamma listened at the door, and heard her sobbing.

"Susy!" said she; "do you want to come out?" "No, mamma," said Susy. "I am not better enough, yet."

Then she heard her mamma going away from the closet-door, and it was very silent in the nursery, for Robbie had been carried down stairs. But Susy was not all alone. Aunt Patience was with her in the dark closet, and so was the little angel, Faith.

"I am the naughtiest child in the world," said Susy.

"But God loves you and He will forgive you," said Faith.

"Are there any children in heaven who used to be as naughty as I am?"

"I don't know," said Faith. "You might ask your mother."

Then Susy burst into tears again.

"I don't believe there are!" said she.

"But God can make you good," said Faith.

"Yes, but it takes time," said Aunt Patience. "You must keep trying and trying, and keep praying and praying, and by and by—"

"You'll be an angel," said Faith.

"Susy!" said her mamma, "are you good, now?"

"Yes, mamma, I guess I'm get

ting good," said Susy in a little meek voice.

Then her mamma opened the door, and took her in her arms and kissed her. And Robbie came and laid his little sunny head on her lap, and said, for he only knew a few words: "My Susy!"

And Susy began to cry again.

"Mamma!" said she at last, "do you think there are any children in heaven as naughty as I am?"

"Yes!" said her mamma. "I think there are a great many."

"How did they get there?"

"Jesus carried them. He loves to forgive little children. And they are not naughty after they get there."

Then the little angel Faith smiled, and was pleased. And Susy said in her heart: "I will try to be good, and mind God. I am sorry I was angry. I will try to be like Jesus."

By this time she looked pale and tired, and Mrs. Love pitied her. She sat rocking her in her lap till she fell asleep, and her mamma watched her and prayed for her silently in her heart. Nobody heard her but God.

She was asking him to forgive her poor little Susy, and make her gentle and mild, like Jesus.

CHAPTER VIII.

ONE very cold day, about two months after Christmas, Susy was playing with a little village. Her mamma noticed that every time any of the things fell down, she gave a little impatient cry.

"I'm afraid Susy isn't well," said she to herself. Towards night Susy put her hand up to her head, and cried out: "O my head! my head!" Her mamma took her up, and felt of her hands. They were very hot. She saw that her face was quite red.

"I will put your feet in hot water," said she; "and you shall go to bed. And perhaps you will feel better by and by." So she carried Susy up into the nursery and soaked her feet, and after she had put her into her crib, she said: "Now I am going to give you a ride into my room. You are going to sleep by me to-night."

Susy tried to smile, but she felt too sick. Her mamma felt very uneasy; but she went to the wash-stand and wet a cloth in water, to lay on Susy's head. When Susy saw what she was going to do, she said: "I wouldn't do so, dear."

She was so sick that she called her mamma "dear."

"It may make your head feel better," said her mamma.

"Well!" said Susy.

But in the morning she was a great deal sicker, and her papa went to good Dr. Merton, and said to him: "My little Susy is very sick. I wish you would come and see her."

When Dr. Merton came, he said to Susy: "Where do you feel sick, Susy?"

"Everywhere," said Susy. "My head feels sick, and my arms feel sick. And I have been slapped all over." She meant that she felt sore and tired:

"I think she will have a fever," said the doctor. Then he told her mamma what to do for her, and went away. After he had gone, the little angel Faith went up to Susy and they whispered together some time.

The next day Susy said to her mamma: "If I get much sicker I think I shall die."

"Do you want to die, dear Susy?" said her mamma.

"My poor little head won't

ache up there! My lips won't be sore up there! I shall never be naughty up there!"

"Would you go and leave poor mamma?"

It hurt Susy to turn over. She had been lying with her face to the wall, but she now turned over, stretched out her hand, and said:

"I will let you go with me, you dear little mamma!"

Then her mamma could not help crying. She said to herself

"I love my little Susy dearly. I don't know what I should do, if she should die. But she would be very happy in heaven. I will ask God to do just as he thinks best."

Then she heard Susy and Faith talking to each other.

"If I go to heaven I shall see Jesus," said Susy.

"And your dear grandmamma, too."

"Yes, and my little cunning little uncle Robbie."

"And perhaps God will let you come flying down to get the souls of little dead babies and carry them up to heaven."

"Mamma, I am vely tired," said Susy; "oh! so tired!"

Then Aunt Patience came and stood by the crib and never moved away for many weeks. She bathed Susy's hot head, she helped her bear the hard pain, she made her try to comfort her mamma.

"Mamma! don't you want to

lie down? Mamma, don't I tire you?" Susy would ask many times every day. "Mamma! are you too tired to wet my lips?"

At last the doctor said, one morning:

"Susy is better. She is going to get well." And as he was going down stairs he met Sarah, the cook, who looked at him, as much as to say: "How is she?"

"She is better," said the doctor.

"Oh! I'm so glad!" said Sarah. 'For she has been so patient! You can't think!" And Sarah put her apron right over her head, and began to cry.

The next day Robbie was allowed to come in and look at Susy. He did not know what had become of her. He stood up on tiptoe and peeped at her through the bars of her crib, and made signs to her to get up and play with him. Miss Joy had been away on a journey all the time Susy had been sick. But now she came back, bag and baggage, with ever so many toys and books that she had been saving till Susy got well. She peeped through the bars, too, and smiled, and Susy smiled, and held out her hand, as much as to say:

"How do you do, Miss Joy? Where have you been?"

"Oh! I always go away when you are in trouble," said Miss Joy.

"'Then you are not so good as Mrs. Love," said Susy; "for she never goes away or leaves me when I am sick."

CHAPTER IX.

WHILE Susy was sick, her mamma and Mrs. Love and Aunt Patience, never left her. They were all the time doing something to comfort her. But now she was getting well fast, and felt very weak and tired, and Mrs. Patience often went away, and then Susy would cry, and fret, and make her mamma take her up, and lay her down, and carry her about, all day long. She would not let her go out of her sight, without crying. Now you must not blame her for this. You must remember how feeble she was, and how sick she had been; and don't you know how you behaved when you had the measles?

One morning Susy's mamma put a pillow in a low chair, and took her up and dressed her in a pink dressing-gown, that she had made on purpose for her to wear when she was sick. Then she combed her hair. Most of it had been cut off when Susy was sick, and what little was left, was all matted together. Then she placed the small table that Susy had for her last birth-day present in front of the chair, and on the table she put a cup and saucer, a plate, a tea-pot, a cream-pitcher, and a sugar-bowl. These had just been brought to Susy by a kind friend

Susy after her Sickness.—P. 78, 1st Series.

Teachers.

who did not know she had been sick.

Susy looked at her mamma, as she moved about, getting her breakfast ready, but did not say a word. She could not talk half so much now, as she could before the fever left her, for she was very weak.

At last her mamma said: "Susy, why don't you ask me where this pretty tea-set came from?" "I don't know," said Susy, faintly.

"Oh! you are too tired to talk, darling. Mamma did not know how weak you were. You shall have your breakfast; then you will feel better."

So some nice, soft toast was brought in, and Susy ate a large slice, and then another small slice, and drank two cups of milk and water. By that time she was so refreshed that she began to admire her new cups and saucers, and she wanted Robbie to come in and see them. Robbie came in with Susy's great doll in his arms. Susy seemed glad to see her doll once more, and in the course of the day she played a little with it.

So the next day her mamma said to her:

"Now my dear little Susy, I want you to spare mamma a little while. I want to go and see Mrs. Wilson, whose baby is very sick. You can have dolly get into bed with you. I won't be gone long."

On hearing this, Susy began to cry.

"Susy, dear, if you were very sick, and going to die, don't you think Mrs. Wilson would come to see me?"

"Would it comfort you, if she came?"

"Yes, it would. And I want to go and comfort her, because pretty soon she won't have any little baby."

"Let your mamma go, Susy,

like a good girl," said Mrs. Love. "I'll stay with you while she is gone."

"Yes," said Mr. Ought, "let her go."

"Do go, dear mamma," said Susy. "I know you won't be gone long from your sick child!"

Her mamma smiled, and Mr. Ought said to her: "Susy, you and I are getting to be very good friends. One of these days, if you have a little Susy of your own, I will be her friend too, and will help her to be a comfort to you."

Susy smiled, and began to think so hard about having a little Susy of her own, that she was surprised when her mamma came back, to see her so soon.

"Did you see the little baby, mamma?"

"Yes, I saw it. It is very sick. It is going to die."

"When it is dead will they bury it in the ground?"

"Yes, darling."

"And then will they go home, and leave it all alone?"

"Susy, I once read a very sweet sentence about that. I will repeat it to you. 'It is not we that go home, and leave our friends behind; no, it is they that are gone to the better home and left us behind.' That dear little baby will get home before its mamma."

"Home to heaven," said the angel Faith, drawing nigh.

"I should think it would be pretty glad when it got there," said Susy. "I suppose it would be looking round to see if Mr. Pain had got to heaven too. And when it found he hadn't, it would be pretty glad."

CHAPTER X.

THOUGH Susy was now able to be dressed every day, she was still feeble, and her mamma spent most of the time in amusing her. Sometimes she held her in her arms and sang all sorts of funny things out of Mother Goose, to make her laugh. Sometimes she told her stories about what she used to do when she was a little girl. And sometimes they would get to talking and laughing about Miss Joy, Mrs. Love, and Susy's other teachers.

One day Susy was more restless than usual. She did not like to lie in bed, or to sit up. She was tired of being rocked, and of being drawn about the room in her little carriage.

"Mamma," said she, "don't you remember how uncle Henny used to carry Robbie, right in his hands?"

"With Robbie's head leaning against his breast? Yes, I remember. Do you think it would rest you if I should carry you so?"

"Yes, mamma, if you feel better enough."

Then her mamma made a chair of her two hands, and Susy sat on the chair, with her head leaning back. It felt very comfortable.

"I've carried you and Robbie

a good many miles in this way," said her mamma.

"Both at once?"

"Oh! no; one at a time, when you were babies. And it was in the night, when other folks were asleep."

"Tell me more, dear mamma."

"Did I ever tell you about the catnip tea that I scalded my hands with? Oh! then I must tell you now. Robbie was not well. Mr. Pain was hurting him."

"Oh! did Robbie have a Mr. Pain?" said Susy.

"Yes, he had him indeed. Well, Robbie was to have some catnip tea, and I put it on the fire to warm. And while it was warming I kept rocking Robbie and singing to him, and all at once he fell asleep. Just then the catnip tea began to boil. I looked at Robbie to see if it would do to lay him down, and found he was only half-asleep. While I waited, the tea kept boiling, and I began to be afraid it would boil over and put out my fire. Then I looked at Robbie, and he began to open his eyes. I was sure he would wake up and cry, if I tried to lay him down, and I was afraid to take the catnip tea off the fire, because it was so hot and I had only one hand to do it with. You know Robbie lay on the other arm. But at last, just as it was going to boil over, I took hold of the cup and was lifting it gently off the fire, when Robbie woke up and gave my hand a little jerk, so that the hot tea flew all over it."

"How did it feel?"

"Not very nice. Mr. Pain made my fingers smart."

"Oh! did you have a Mr. Pain, mamma?"

"Yes, I had one. And I've a Mr. Pain now. He's pushing a pin right into my side just under your head. If you could move your head a little bit, I could get it out."

Susy moved her head, and the pin was pulled out. By this time she felt quite rested. She had forgotten all her discomfort. It doesn't take much to amuse little folks.

"If you had a Mr. Pain, I suppose you had a Mr. Ought," said Susy. "Did you like him, mamma?"

"I don't think I liked him very well at first. But that was because I did not know him."

"I suppose you always minded him."

"No, I remember very well that I often disobeyed him. And then he used to follow me about, and would not give me any peace."

"Mamma!" cried Susy, sitting up quite straight, "don't you wish you was a little girl, like me?

And then we could play together with my blocks. You could hand me the blocks, and I could build a house with them!"

"Oh! if you feel able to build a house, I can hand you the blocks. If I were a little girl, perhaps we should quarrel. Perhaps I should want you to hand me the blocks and let me build the house."

Susy smiled. She felt a great deal better. The walking and the talking had rested her. And now it was time for her dinner, and Nurse came in to bring it. Robbie came too, and while Susy was eating her chicken-broth he watched her, and looked as if he wanted some too.

"Give him a little, do." said Mrs. Love.

"It isn't good for him," said Susy. "I'm afraid it would hurt him."

"Oh! let him have one taste, do."

"It would burn his mouth."

"You might blow it, then."

"I don't believe he wants any."

All this time Susy kept eating as fast as she could, and wishing Robbie would go away, and not stand there, looking so good and lovely. But it wouldn't do!

"There! he shall have some, little dear!" she said at last. And she held out her spoon, and Robbie opened his rosy mouth just like a young bird, while she fed him, and she felt as happy as if she were the great mother-bird and not just little Susy Miller!

CHAPTER XI.

It was cold, wintry weather when Susy was taken sick, but it was beginning to be spring when she was well enough to go out of doors. Her papa would not trust any one else to take her, the first time she rode out. He put her, on a pillow, into her little carriage, and drew her round the square. By the time they got back to the house again, Susy was so tired that she wanted to go in. But the next day she rode round the square twice, and her papa carried her, in his arms, up and down the yard, besides. As she lay with her head on his shoulder, she often said: "Do I tire you, dear papa?"

And then he would laugh, and say she didn't weigh so much as a little kitten, and he could carry a big kitten all day.

"Papa!" said Susy, at last, "mamma says Mr. Pain has made me a pretty long visit."

"Yes, it was pretty long."

"Don't you hope he never will come again, papa?"

"I don't know. He has taught my little Susy so many good lessons, that I shall want him to come and teach me, next news."

Susy thought this very funny.

"Why, what could he teach you, papa? Don't you know every thing?"

"Oh! he might teach me to think of other people, more than of myself. If my papa were carrying me about, he might put it into my head to ask him every now and then: "Don't I tire you?"

"Papa, you are a funny man," said Susy. "You are almost as funny as mamma."

"I'm a pretty good horse, I think," said her papa. "See how I can trot."

Susy laughed, and looked up to the nursery-window to see if Robbie were in sight. Yes, there was his little smiling face close to the glass.

"O papa! put me down now; please, papa! And give Robbie a ride. Robbie has got four great big teeth coming, and he doesn't feel nice, at all."

Her papa kissed her, and carried her up stairs, and she sat in Robbie's chair, and looked down into the yard, and saw her papa be a horse and trot up and down with the merry little fellow on his back. She felt very happy, indeed, because she had given him so much pleasure. But she was tired, and her head ached a little.

"My headache aches," said she to Nurse.

"I should think it would, with that thick hood on this warm day You are nothing but a big bun dle. Come! I'll take off your things, and you shall sit in my lap, and I'll—let me see; what shall I do? oh! I'll tell you about Robbie."

"What about him?" asked Susy.

"Why, how he behaved when you were sick. Don't you think he wouldn't eat any thing, at first. He would go and get your chair ready for you, and climb up into his; and then he would sit waiting for you to come. His dinner would get as cold as a stone before he would touch it. One day he slipped into your mamma's room and tried to pull you out of your crib, and when he found you took no notice of him, he came back and got the hearth-brush, and tried to get you up by pushing it through the bars."

"I suppose he thought I was a ball," said Susy.

"I dare say he did," said Nurse.

"For he always gets his ball from under the sofa, with the hearth-brush."

"Can't you think of something else?" asked Susy.

"Why, yes," said Nurse, "I was going to ask you if you wouldn't like to come back and get your dinner and supper with him, he grieves so for you."

"On my little table?"

"Yes."

"With my new cups and saucers? He would break my new cups and saucers all to pieces."

"Well, it's no matter. I only thought as he is such a little dear, and his teeth tease him so—"

"Such a sweet little darling!" said Mrs. Love.

"That you would like to come back and eat with him," said Nurse.

"Well, I will," said Susy. "I'll come back to supper. And I'll let him pour out tea, and I'll let him sit on my cushion."

"You see he is such a little fellow," said Mrs. Love. "And so good, and gentle! And he loves you so, dearly!"

So Susy told her mamma she was going to eat with Robbie now, and for answer she got a sweet kiss.

It was not long before Susy became strong enough to go, with her mamma, into the country, where she staid all summer, and grew quite plump and rosy Robbie and Mrs. Love, and Miss Joy and Mr. Ought and the angel Faith went, too, but they were not sure whether Mr. Pain went or not. Susy said she saw his rod in his mamma's trunk, but she might have been mistaken, you know.

"So they all played together."—P. 7, 2d Series.

Servants

LITTLE SUSY'S

SIX TEACHERS.

BY HER

AUNT SUSAN

NEW-YORK

1864.

LITTLE SUSY'S SIX TEACHERS.

CHAPTER I.

THINGS went on, after Susy's visit to the country, pretty much as they did before. Mrs. Love had to send for Mr. Pain now and then, to come and give Susy a little slap on her arm, just to remind her that he was alive, and ready when he was wanted. You see it was Mrs. Love who was so fond of Susy, and so tender and gentle, who sent for Mr. Pain, and the reason is this. She knew that Susy could not be happy unless she was good, and that it was easier to suffer a little from Mr. Pain now, than by and by to suffer from ill-temper, disobedience, and self-will.

One day grandmamma sent for Susy and Robbie to come and spend the day with her. She lived in the country, not far from New-York, and they all loved to go there. Frank and Charlie, Susy's cousins, were invited, too; and they got there first. Charlie was shy. He was not used to playing with girls, and so he thought he did not like them. When he saw Susy coming, he put on his cap and said: "Good by, grandma. If girls are coming, I must go. I can't stay where there are girls."

"You can't go without me,' said Frank, "and I am sure I shan't go."

Charlie was obliged to content himself with hiding behind his grandma; but after a while he began to peep out, and look at Susy, and at last concluded he would play with her, as it couldn't be helped.

"I've decided to play with her," said he to Frank. "I'm sorry she's a girl, but now I've decided I shan't change my mind." Now I ought to tell you that when this happened, Charlie was between three and four years old. Susy was a little older than Charlie, but Charlie was taller and stronger, and knew more than she did.

So they all played together, and Robbie sat on his nurse's lap and watched them, for he was not big enough to be trusted long away from her. Susy's great doll had come to see grandma, with the other children. Susy said she was sick and needed change of air. After they had played till they were tired, Frank found a book, and sat down to read Robbie went to take his nap, and Susy petted her doll, and began to make believe give it medicine. Now Charlie did not like dolls, and he tried to think of some means to get Miss Peggy out of the way.

"If she's so sick, she'll die pretty soon," said he. "Oh! I guess she won't die," said Susy. "She's taken twenty ten pills, and ever so much castor-oil, and a dose of—a dose of—well, I don't know what it was, but something dreadful."

"Let me see her," said Charlie. "Oh! she's dead. She's all dead. We'll bury her."

"Well, so we will!" cried Susy.

So they each took a stick and began to dig a hole in the midst of grandma's garden. When they had dug a pretty large one, they squeezed Miss Peggy down into it, and covered her with leaves.

"Now she's dead and buried," said Charlie, "let's go and think about her. People always sit down and think about dead folks."

So they sat down and looked very grave for some minutes, when Susy said:

"There! I've thoughted an hour, and now I am going to take her up."

"No, you musn't. She's dead.

And we ought to wear black. I am her father. and you are her mother."

Susy was just going to cry. "I don't want my dear dolly to be dead any longer," said she.

"If you are going to cry, I guess I'll go home," said Charlie. "I don't like girls very well."

Just then, Nurse, who had heard all their little talk, came down.

"Dolly isn't dead," said she.

"She's only muddy. You musn't bury her again."

"What for musn't I?" asked Susy.

"Because it gets her all muddy. And dollies don't like to be buried. It makes them feel quite discouraged to be buried."

"Then I won't do so again," said Susy.

CHAPTER II.

When the children were going home, grandma said she wanted them all to come again, when her fruit would be ripe. So one pleasant day in September they all met there; Susy and Robbie, Frank and Charlie, and both their mammas.

In the afternoon, as they were playing under the trees, Robbie picked up some plums.

"Nice pums!" said he.

"Robbie musn't eat them," said Susy.

Robbie would mind even Susy. He had a little pocket in his apron, and so, instead of eating the plums, he filled his pocket. When they began to play again, the plums were crushed, and the juice ran all over his apron. When they went in, his mamma asked Susy how it had happened. Susy did not know. She thought he had been eating the plums.

"He has been eating plums,' said she. "I tolded him not to eat them, and he did."

"No! no! Robbie no no eat pums," said Robbie. Susy looked at him very sorrowfully.

"Robbie has told a naughty story," said she. "And I am afraid he'll have to be tookened to that bad old place."

This was a little, dark closet under the stairs, where Susy had once seen a lady shut up her son for telling an untruth. After that she always thought it had been built on purpose for boys who told falsehoods.

"Did you see Robbie eat the plums?" asked her mamma.

"No, mamma. He was going to eat them, and I tolded him not to. And then we were playing, and I didn't see him any more."

"Robbie no no eat pums," said Robbie.

"He put them in his pocket; I saw him," said Charlie. "And when we rolled on the grass, I guess he squeezed them up."

"Oh! yes," said Mrs. Love, "I dare say that was it. I did not believe dear little Robbie would tell a naughty story."

"I'm glad he didn't!" said Susy. "Robbie wouldn't tell a naughty story, would he?"

Robbie hadn't the least idea what a naughty story was; but

when Susy kissed him, and said that, he smiled and said: "No, no, Robbie, not naughty 'tory." This made them all laugh, and Susy asked her mamma if Robbie might have a plum, because he was such a good boy.

Her mamma said he might have one, if grandma chose to have it picked off the tree for him. Those on the ground were not sweet like those on the tree.

Grandma said he should have a

little basket full, and she went out and shook the tree, and the children filled a basket which used to hold strawberries. Then, without waiting to be told, Robbie offered some of the plums to every body, and when his mamma, just to see what he would say, took the very last one, leaving none for him, there was not a cloud on his little, smiling face, and he went and sat down on the door-step without saying a word.

"O Susy! Robbie hasn't any plum for himself," said Mrs. Love. "The little darling has given every one away. Do give him one of yours."

"I only had three," said Susy. "And one is eaten up. And the other I have bitten. And I was going to keep the other, it is such a big one."

"I think you are very selfish," said Mr. Ought.

Susy made no answer. She ate

the second plum, and began to play with the third, by rolling it on the stone step. When it rolled down she ran after it, and Mr. Ought ran after her.

"Susy!" said he, "Susy! I should think you might give it to Robbie."

"Go away!" said Susy. "I want to play."

Mr. Ought did not stir. Miss Joy, however, ran and hid. Susy felt pretty uncomfortable.

"I'm sure mamma will give him one," said she.

Mr. Ought looked grieved.

"I wish I had one," said Mrs. Love. "I would give it to the dear little generous fellow in a minute."

"Would you?" said Susy. "I've a good mind to give him mine. It is a big one, though, and mamma meant he should have a little one."

While she was waiting she saw

her mamma take Robbie up and kiss him, and heard her say: 'Here, Robbie, darling, is your plum. Mamma would not eat it for the world. And here is another one that grandma sent you, besides."

Then Robbie smiled, and looked pleased, and Susy wished she had given him hers, and then she would have had that sweet smile, and Miss Joy wouldn't have run away, and Mr. Ought wouldn't have teased her so, but would have called her "Good Susy!"

She came and sat down by Robbie, looking very disconsolate.

Her mamma guessed her thoughts.

"Never mind, dear," said she, "Robbie has as many now, as are good for him. And I know you love him, and often give him things. And next time you won't be selfish, I know."

CHAPTER III.

THE reason Susy's mamma said that was this. Susy was very apt to think herself worse than other children, and when she fancied herself very bad, she almost always grew bad. She would think there was no use in trying to be good, and as soon as she stopped trying, why it was very easy to be naughty.

The next day Susy was invited to spend with Charlie and Frank. It was Saturday, and Frank was to be at home from school. When she woke in the morning, Mr. Ought said to her: "Now Susy, God has taken care of you all night. Kneel down and thank him, the very first thing you do."

"I don't think God can hear me, very well," said Susy. "There are a great many folks praying to him. I guess I'd better wait till by and by. He won't be so busy, by and by."

"Oh! he can hear you just as well now," said the little angel Faith.

"I don't believe it," said Susy. "And I want to go down and get my breakfast."

Susy ran down stairs, and, as she had neglected her dear Father in heaven, it was not strange that she now was so careless as not to bid her grandmamma good-morning.

But her grandmamma was too much like Mrs. Love to find fault with Susy. She only said in a pleasant voice:

"Susy has forgotten her grandma, hasn't she?"

After breakfast Susy went to walk with Robbie and nurse, and on the way home, they left her at her aunty's.

Frank and Charley had been watching for her some time, and they both ran down to meet her, and Frank kissed her over and over, and kept saying he wished she was his little sister. Then they all went up into the nursery, and Charley showed Susy all his toys and books. Susy liked to lie flat on the floor and look at books, and as soon as she found how many there were, she threw herself down, and began to look at the pictures.

After a while, Charley said: "Come, Susy, let's go out and play now."

"Oh! no, I wouldn't," said Susy.

Charley waited, and waited. At last he got quite out of patience.

"I don't like girls," said he. "They never do any thing you want them to."

Susy took no notice of what he said, but kept on turning over the books.

"You can't have my books any longer," he said at last. He began to gather them up, and to put them away in his book-case. Susy did not care, so long as he left her the book at which she was looking; but when he tried to take that, she held on fast, and he began to pull it very hard to get it away. He was stronger than Susy, and in a minute or two, he had the book in his hands. But one cover was nearly torn off.

"Now you've spoiled my book," said Frank. "You have just spoiled it."

"It was Charlie, pulling it away from me," said Susy.

"It was Susy, holding on, so," said Charlie. "I did not know it was your book, though. I thought it was mine. But I don't care."

"I don't care, either," said Susy.

"I'll make you care, then," said Frank who was by this time, quite angry. And he leaned over and slapped them with the cover they had torn off. The moment he had done it he ran to his mother, and told her what had happened.

"You struck your little cousin, and your little brother?" said his mother, hardly able to believe him.

"Yes, I did. And I feel better for it," said Frank.

His mother was astonished.

"Why, Frank," said she, "if any one else had told me this, I would not have believed it!"

"They provoked me so!" said Frank. "If they hadn't said they didn't care, I shouldn't have been so angry. But after they had torn my book, they said they didn't care."

"If they had been grown up, it would have been wrong for you to do as you did," said his mother. "But as they are only foolish little children, not yet four years old, you have behaved ridiculously, and done wrong besides."

Frank began to agree with his mother.

"I'll go back and make up with them," said he. "They both sit there crying on the floor. I am sorry I struck them."

"That's right!" said his mother. So Frank ran back to the nursery, and told Susy he was sorry he had hurt her; and Susy said it was no matter, and Charlie said it would take more than Frank to hurt him, and so by degrees they forgave each other, and that was the end of their quarrel.

When Susy was going to bed that night, she said to Mr. Ought: "I have been rather naughty to day. But I mean to be rather good to-morrow, if you only will be kind to me, and not keeping saying 'Susy!' all the time."

"If you had obeyed me yesterday about the plum, all your trouble would have been over, then. But you would not give

Robbie one, when you had three," said Mr. Ought.

"Oh! I was afraid it would hurt him," said Susy.

"No, that was not the reason."

"Yes, it was."

Mr. Ought was silent. Susy knelt down to say her prayers, but they did not comfort her. Presently Mr. Ought said: "The reason you kept all the plums was, that you loved little Susy better than you loved little Robbie.

And as you would not listen to me then, you found it hard to listen to me this morning. And so you were very selfish at your Aunty's, and made Frank so angry. You see how it is. If you disobey me once you will find it easy to disobey me again."

"I haven't had a very good time to-day," said Susy. "I have not seen Miss Joy once. I think I'm a pretty bad child."

"No little girl ever became good in a minute," said Aunt Patience."

"But I want to," said Susy.

"Ask God to help you," said Faith. "And then He will let me help you," said Aunt Patience.

"Well!" said Susy, "I will turn over a new leaf, to-morrow."

CHAPTER IV.

Little children often "turn over a new leaf." After being more or less naughty for several weeks, they will, all of a sudden, have a fit of goodness and be quite lovely. It was so with Susy. She woke the next day, which was Sunday, feeling very sweet and pleasant, and could not help shaking hands with Mr. Ought before she went down to breakfast.

"Mr. Ought!" said she, "should you think I would be glad it is Sunday?"

"Yes, I should think you would," said Mr. Ought.

"I haven't told any body whether I'm glad, or not. It's a secret," said Susy. "But I know one thing. When Rob gets big enough to go to church, and I can feel him taking hold of my hand, and he can walk along with me, and sit by me in the pew, I guess I shall like Sunday better than I do now."

"Of course," said Mrs. Love.

Susy went to church with her papa and mamma in the morning. She was generally a very good girl at church. She was even better than usual at this time, and when they got home, her papa told her a beautiful story from the Bible, and he kissed her, and said

"What a comfort it is to have a child who tries to be good!"

In the afternoon nurse went to church and their mamma staid with Robbie and Susy, and they sang hyms, and heard stories till Robbie all at once fell fast asleep in his chair.

"The little darling!" said Mrs. Love. "He was tired: he shall go and lie on the sofa and have a nap."

While he was asleep, Susy sat in her mamma's lap, and as she was tired of hearing stories and of singing, they had a little talk together.

"Susy, you were a very good girl at church this morning."

"How could I be naughty, mamma?"

"Oh! in a great many ways. One child could disturb fifty people."

"What could it do."

"It could keep getting up and down on its seat. It could keep asking if service was almost done. It could turn over the leaves of the hymn-book and rattle them. It could gape, and yawn, and fidget. It could try to make some other child laugh. Or it might turn round and look right into other people's faces in a rude way."

Susy had seen children do all these things. Mr. Ought whispered that she had done some of them herself.

"Mamma," said she "it is hard to sit still."

"I know it is, and that is one reason why it is good for you to go to church. You know you must sit still, and you try to learn to do it. And it is well to learn to do hard things."

"What for do little children go to church?" asked Susy. "They don't know what the minister says."

"No, I know they don't understand much. But there are a good many reasons why they should go to church, even then. I can not explain them all to such a little girl as you are. But one reason is this. If they always go when they are children, they will be likely to go when they are grown up. Besides, nobody goes there just to hear what the minister says. We go to worship God. Even little Susy can please and honor Him by just sitting still in

His house, and making no noise. And some of the blessing he has for the grown people, he showers down on the little ones who are brought there to get it."

Susy smiled.

"I'll sit still, and may be he'll shower some on me," said she.

"You needn't say may be," said Faith. "You may say, He certainly will."

CHAPTER V.

AT last Susy had a real trouble. Her aunt Maria moved away from New-York, and went to live in the country, near grandmamma. Susy now could not see Frank and Charlie every week, and she missed them very much indeed. She cried so much when she went to bid them good-by that, in order to comfort her, her Aunty invited her to go with them.

"That would make too much trouble," said Susy.

"Oh! yes, just as you are moving," said her mamma. "But if Susy is very good, and you would like a visit from her after you are nicely settled in your new house, I should like her to go." So in a few weeks Susy went. But she staid at her grandmamma's, and slept all by herself in a little room that grandma kept on purpose for the children when they came to see her. Then Frank and Charlie came to see Susy, or she went to see them, every day. When she had been there two weeks, her mamma and Robbie came for her. But grandmamma would not let her go.

Susy had become such a gentle, affectionate little girl that it was a pleasure to have her in the house, and then grandma was so much like Mrs. Love, that she was not very ready to see faults in any one, especially not in little folks. So they all staid another week, and a very happy week it was.

When Susy and Robbie, and their mamma, went back to their own home, they begged Aunt Maria to come and make them a visit, with Frank and Charlie.

"I do not think I can go this fall," said she. "But in the spring perhaps I can."

"Oh! go now, Aunty, do," said Susy.

"No, dear, not now. It would not be convenient now."

Susy was just beginning to say: "O Aunty! do come?" when she remembered that she had often been told that it is not proper for children to tease their friends to do things they have just refused to do.

"How many years will it be before spring?" she asked.

Her Aunty smiled. "It will only be a few months," said she. "Not more than five or six."

Susy did not know much about time. However, as there was no help for it, she had to wait, and Aunt Patience told her she would stay with her and make the time fly quite fast.

But as soon as they were all nicely settled at home, Susy began to expect her aunt and cousins. Every time the door-bell rang she would say: "Oh! there they are!" and when she found herself mistaken she would laugh, and say: "Aunt Patience! how much longer shall I have to wait?"

At last Aunt Maria wrote, to say that Frank and Charlie had the whooping-cough, and would not be able to come.

"Would it catch me if I went there?" asked Susy.

"You would catch it," said her nurse, smiling.

So it was a whole year before Aunt Maria found it convenient to make the promised visit, and Susy was then a little more than five and Robbie three years old. They were all very happy to meet again.

"Why, Susy! how you have grown!" said Frank.

"Yes, papa marks me on the wall, so as to make me grow," said Susy.

"Isn't she a funny little thing?"

said Frank. He kept kissing her and trying to take her up and carry her. But Susy held back. She felt too big to be carried, and she felt a little shy, too, for Frank had altered a good deal since she had seen him, and then he kept looking at her so!

"O mother! I wish I had a little sister," said he.

"I don't," said Charlie.

"Charlie would love her, if he had one." said his mother. "But now, as he isn't used to girls, he fancies he doesn't like them."

Just then Mrs. Love whispered to Susy. She said: "I should think you would take your cousins up to see dear little Robbie."

"Oh! don't you want to go up stairs, and see Robbie?" said Susy.

"I forgot all about Robbie," said Frank. "Where is he? I suppose he won't know me, but we'll soon get acquainted."

They all ran up to the nursery, where they found Robbie standing at a chair in which was a bowl of water. He was all undressed.

When he saw the three children come flying in, he looked down at his two little hands that lay flat on the bottom of the bowl, and did not move or speak.

"Why, Robbie! don't you know Cousin Frank?" said Susy. "He's such a little fellow he doesn't know how to behave. He's afraid of strangers. Won't Robbie say his hymn to sister Susy?"

Robbie looked solemnly at his hands, and did not speak, but he peeped out from under his great long eye-lashes, at Frank and Charlie.

"You ought not to come and hinder me when I am dressing Robbie," said his nurse. "I was going to dress him up before his aunty saw him."

"But I want him to say his hymn," said Susy.

"You'll have to wait till he gets acquainted," said his nurse.

"Well, we'll go down then," said Frank, and they all three ran off, while little Miss Joy flew after them, quite out of breath with delight.

"Of course they've left the door wide open," said Nurse. "I never saw such children."

Nurse always said this, no matter what they did. But most people have seen just such children, and have had to shut the door after them a hundred, perhaps a thousand times.

When Robbie was dressed he was taken down to see his aunty, who had been wondering why he did not come. She had a little horse for him. Robbie was very thankful for it, and that night, when he said his prayers, he looked at his horse and said: "O God! send grass!"

CHAPTER VI.

FRANK and Charlie staid several weeks, and during the whole time, there was no quarrelling.

Before their mother would take them from home she made them promise to try to be gentle and obedient, and to do all they could to make Susy and Robbie happy. And Mrs. Love said a good deal to Susy about forgetting herself and trying to please her cousins. "A little girl who loves Jesus, and is like him," said Mrs. Love, "will be kind, and will not be vexed at every trifle. She never will envy others, thinking people love them better than they do her, or give them better things. She does not spend her time in pleasing herself, nor is she easily provoked. It is hard to make her believe any thing evil of others, and when she sees them do wrong, she never is glad."

"Am I such a little girl?" asked Susy.

"Mr. Ought can tell you," said Mrs. Love.

Mr. Ought gave his answer in a whisper. Nobody heard it but Susy.

"You can be such a little girl," said Faith.

The children could not play out of doors much of the time, for the weather was cold and damp. But they amused themselves with their toys and books, and the time flew away very fast. One afternoon two little boys who lived near, came to stay a few hours. Their names were George and Willie. Their mamma had been dead ever since they could remember, and they were sometimes invited to come and see Susy. Frank and Charlie were a little younger than they were.

"You may play in the attic," said Susy's mamma. "I am going out with Aunt Maria, and shall feel easier to have you there, than out of doors."

So they all ran up, making a great noise with their boots, at least the four boys did, and Susy said they would have a swing.

Just then Robbie's little feet were heard on the stairs, and his little pleasant voice, saying:

"My Susy! I'm 'toming up!"

"He'll be in our way," said George.

"Yes, he'll be in our way," said Susy. But just then Mrs. Love said to her, gently: "Susy, dear, do you love these four boys better than your little brother?"

"I'll take care of him," said Susy.

"I wish you would," said Nurse, "for he feels lonesome down in the nursery, when he hears you all playing up here."

Susy had to watch Robbie very carefully. He kept running before the swing; and she was afraid he would be thrown down. Do you think it was easy for her to do this, just as she was expecting to have a good play with her little friends? No, it was not easy. You should love her for it, and do as she did.

George was a selfish boy. When he saw what Susy was doing, he laughed, and said he was glad he hadn't any little babies to take care of. But Frank said

"Let's play something Robbie can play. He isn't a baby. He is three years old. What can he play, Susy?"

"He can play horse," said Susy.

"Then we'll play horse with him," said Frank.

"And he shall be the driver, and we'll be the horses."

"I don't like to be a horse," said Charlie. "I'd rather be the man, and say: 'Get up.'"

"Robbie doesn't care whether

he's the horse or the man," said Susy.

But Frank persuaded Charlie to let Robbie be the man, and then he and Susy and Charlie and Willie were horses, and Robbie drove them all round the attic till they were out of breath.

He was so happy that they all felt repaid for what little trouble he had made them. His nurse now came for him, and he went down with her.

"Now you shall all be robbers, and I will try to catch you and put you in jail," said George.

"That would be first-rate fun," said Frank. "We ought each to have a den to live in."

"Those big trunks would make good dens," said George.

"But they're full of things," said Susy.

"We can take them out, just while we play," said George.

"I am afraid mamma would not like it."

"She won't know it," said George. "When we've done playing we can put the things back again. She'll never know it."

Susy looked at the trunks. She thought it would be delightful to be a robber and have a big trunk for her den. But then, was it right to tumble her mamma's things out on the floor without leave?

"No!" said Mr. Ought, "it is not right."

"We musn't do it," said Susy, "without leave."

"You are afraid your mother will whip you, I suppose," said George. "But she won't know any thing about it, so what's the use of being afraid?"

"She wouldn't whip me," said Susy. "But she would say it wasn't right. But I'll ask Nurse if we may. Perhaps Nurse will know."

"Oh! yes, do ask her!" said

Frank. "It would be such fun!"

"She shan't go," said George. "I know that old nurse will say No, just to tease us."

"Run, Susy!" said Frank.

Susy ran, and George ran to prevent her. Her foot caught in the string with which they had been playing horse, and she fell across one of the trunks which Willie and Charlie, not noticing the dispute, had dragged from its corner.

"Oh! I'm killed! I'm dead!" cried she.

George and Willie, on hearing this, ran down stairs, and out of the house, as fast as they could. Frank lifted Susy up, and kissed her, and begged her not to cry, while with his handkerchief he wiped the blood that was running down over her face. She had cut a little place in her cheek. Charlie was very sorry, and very much frightened. He did not know what to do. At last he ran down into the nursery and said in a loud voice:

"Susy's killed and dead!"

CHAPTER VII.

On hearing this dreadful news, poor little Robbie's heart came near breaking in two. His nurse ran up to see what was really the matter, and Robbie threw himself down on the floor, and began to cry very softly, but very mournfully, as if he never meant to get done.

"What's the matter?" said

Nurse to Susy. "Charlie says you are dead!"

"No, I am only most dead," said Susy. "And one of my legs is broken all to pieces. I know it is. I can't move it a bit."

Nurse lifted her up, and carried her down.

"I'll lay you on my bed," said she, "and then we'll see how many pieces you're broken into. That leg is whole; and so is that one."

"It's my ankle," said Susy.

"Oh! I guess you have sprained it," said Frank. "I guess it's nothing but a sprain."

"You wouldn't call it nothing if you had it," said Susy.

She kept on crying, and making a great ado, till all at once Aunt Patience came and sat down on the side of the bed.

"Susy, dear," said she, "don't cry so. Try to bear the pain quietly, or it will make you sick.

Come! sit in my lap, and I will rub your poor ankle, and by and by it will feel better."

"How soon?" asked Susy.

"I don't know. It is swollen a good deal. You may be lame some days. Perhaps all the time Frank and Charlie are here. But what then? Why, Mrs. Love will take good care of you, and Miss Joy will sit by you and make paper babies, and as for me, I will not leave you a minute."

Susy stopped crying. She looked up into the kind face above her, and said: "Do you like to be with sick folks, Aunt Patience?"

"Yes," said Aunt Patience, "I do."

"What can you do for them?"

"I can help them not to scream and cry and make a great uproar. If they have sprained ankles, I help them lie still, and keep quiet till they are better."

"It seems kind of hard," said

Susy, " to have to be lame when Frank and Charlie are here."

" Ah! but don't you remember that you were trying to please me, when you fell?" said Mr. Ought. " Dear Susy! don't you remember that?"

Susy's ankle ached, but her heart was full of joy and peace.

" Oh! there's darling little Robbie lying on the floor, crying!" said she. " Robbie! Robbie! look here!"

"Aren't you all killed and dead?" asked Robbie, lifting up his head.

"No, indeed!" said Susy.

Then Robbie got up, and wiped away his tears, and began to think what he could give her.

At last he remembered his red apple, that his uncle Thomas had sent him.

"You sall have my wed apple," said he.

"Isn't he a little dear?" said

Mrs. Love. "I declare! I don't know which of them is the best!"

"I wish mamma would come home," said Susy. "And I wonder where George and Willie have gone?"

"They've gone home," said her nurse. "I heard them come running down and go out, so I went to the window, and saw them go home. Had you been vexing them?"

"They are not good boys," said Frank.

"That's because they've not been well taught," said Nurse. "There's great excuse to be made for boys who have no mothers."

"I don't like boys that haven't mothers," said Charlie.

"You mean you don't like them if they're bad," said Frank.

"They ought to be good," said Charlie, "because, if their mothers are in heaven, they can look down and see how they behave, and it would make them feel sorry to see their boys naughty."

CHAPTER VIII.

SUSY was lame several weeks. She had to lie on the sofa almost all that time. So she lost much of the pleasure she had expected from the visit of her cousins. Frank was very kind to her, and would sit and read to her a whole hour at a time; and Charlie played about, near the sofa, and amused her a good deal. Miss Joy did not now run away and hide; she sat on the sofa with Susy, and kept her laughing and singing even when she was in pain. Aunt Patience and Mrs. Love were there, too. Every afternoon, when Susy's papa came home, he would tell her such a funny story, or build such remarkable castles on the floor!

When Aunt Maria went home, and told grandmamma how lame Susy was, and how pleasant and patient, you may be sure it was not two days before there came a basket full of good things, such as nobody in the world but a grand-mamma could make.

There were little apple-pies, baked on dolls' plates; babies that were good to eat, because they were dough-nuts; round cakes, and square cakes, and long, narrow cakes! oh! it was a basket indeed!

So on the whole, this was a

very happy time, and then when Susy got well she always had something to date by. That is, she could say, "That happened before I sprained my ankle!" or "Don't you remember, it was about the time I had the sprained ankle?"

But I must hurry on to the end of the story, or you will be tired of Mrs. Love, Miss Joy, Susy, and all of them.

The lame ankle was not the

only wonderful thing that happened to Susy in her fifth year For just before the end of it, that is, just before she became six years old, she heard that something quite as wonderful was going to happen. For Susy's teachers were to have a meeting to report what they had done for her since she became their little scholar, and hear from her papa, whether he wished them to stay six years longer. There was a deal of talk about this meeting, among the teachers. Miss Joy seemed a little uneasy. She said she did not believe they would keep her.

"I never knew how I came to be called a Teacher," said she. "I am only a little, young thing, and I am sure there is some mistake about it. Susy's papa looks pretty grave; I don't believe he likes me. I shall be turned away, I dare say. However, I'll keep up my spirits till I am fairly out of the house. It will be time enough to cry then!" So little Miss Joy was more lively than ever, and made every body laugh.

Mrs. Love said she did not think they could get her out of the house, if they tried; and she felt pretty sure they wouldn't try, as she had been there so long.

Aunt Patience said she did not want to go, at all. But she

would not complain, whatever happened.

Mr. Pain would not say a word, but kept all his thoughts to himself. Susy said if any one was turned away, perhaps he would be that one. But she hoped he wouldn't take that as a hint, and run away till her papa and mamma desired.

Mr. Ought said it would be a sin to send him away, or treat him coldly, but he did not believe

Susy would want him to go now they were such good friends.

The angel Faith did not say much. He had made up his mind to stay, at all events.

CHAPTER IX.

"If Mr. Pain is to be at the meeting, I can't go!" said Miss Joy. She stood on tiptoe before the glass, dressing herself in her holiday clothes.

"Perhaps he would be willing to leave his rod behind him," said Mrs. Love. "I will ask him, at all events."

Mr. Pain thought he should not

feel at home without his rod. He said he always liked to have it in his hand, whether he was to use it, or not.

Miss Joy was full of fun and mischief about this time. So she slipped up slyly behind Mr. Pain, while he was talking, and snatched away the rod before he could turn round. Mrs Love smiled, on seeing this little triek, and they all went down to the parlor and seated themselves with much

" So she slipped up slyly behind Mr. Pain."—P. 98, 2d Series.

Susy's Teachers.

gravity. Little Susy sat in the midst, in her own low chair, looking wide-awake, you may depend. Her papa and mamma sat on each side, like two judges. Mrs. Love rocked herself in the rocking-chair, in a contented, easy way, and Aunt Patience, who liked to do such things, helped Miss Joy to find the leaves of her report, which might have been rose-leaves, they were so small.

Mr. Ought looked very good

indeed, and the angel Faith shone across the room like a sunbeam.

"Susy will be six years old, to-morrow," said her papa. "You have all been teaching her ever since she was born. We will now listen to your reports, and hear what you have taught her, and whether you have done her any good."

They were all silent, but every body looked at Mrs. Love, as much as to say she should begin. Mrs. Love took out a little book with a sky-blue cover and began to read. She was so modest that she had not written much in it, but this is what she read.

"I have not done much for Susy, but love her dearly. And I have not taught her much but to love every body. When she was a baby I tried to teach her to smile, but I don't think I could have taught her if Miss Joy had not helped me. And when she was sick I was always sorry for her, and tried to comfort her."

"You have done her a great deal of good," said Susy's papa. "We will engage you to stay six years longer, should God spare her life."

Then Mr. Pain took up his book. It had a black cover, but the leaves were gilt-edged, and the cover was spangled with stars.

"I have punished Susy a great many times," said Mr. Pain. "Sometimes I slapped her with my hand. Sometimes I struck her with my rod. Sometimes I made her sick. But I never did any of these things because I was angry with her, or liked to hurt her. I only came when Mrs. Love called me."

"You have taught her excellent lessons," said Susy's papa. "If it had not been for you, she would be growing up disobedient and selfish. You may stay six years longer."

Then Mr. Pain made a low bow, and said he was thinking of going away, and sending his brother, Mr. Sorrow, and his sister, Mrs. Disappointment, to take his place.

"Oh! no!" cried Susy's mamma. "Not yet! not yet! Susy is still so little!"

Then Mr. Pain said he would

stay without a rod, as Susy was now too old to be whipped.

Then Miss Joy took up her book with its rainbow covers, and tried to read. But she laughed so heartily all the time, and her leaves kept flying out of her hands at such a rate, that it was not possible to understand what she was saying.

It was all about clapping hands, and running races, and picking flowers, and having a good time. Every body laughed, just because she laughed, and Susy's papa could hardly keep his face grave long enough to say: "You have done more good than tongue can tell. You have made her just such a merry, happy, laughing little creature as I wanted her to be. You must certainly stay six years longer."

Then Mr. Ought drew forth his book. It had silver covers, and its leaves were of the most delicate tissue.

"I have taught little Susy to be good," said he. "Never to touch what is not hers. Never to speak a word that is not true. Never to have a thought she would not like the great and holy God to see. If I stay six years longer, I can teach her a great deal more, for she begins now to understand my faintest whisper. She is such a little girl as I love to live with."

Then Susy turned rosy-red with

pleasure, and her papa and mamma got up and shook hands with Mr. Ought, and begged him never, never, to leave their darling child, as long as she lived.

It was now the turn of Aunt Patience. Her book had covers wrought by her own hands, in grave and gay colors well mingled together.

"When I first came here," said she, "Susy used to cry a great deal whenever she was hurt or punished. When she was sick she was very hard to please. When she sat down to learn to sew, and to read and to write, she would break her thread in anger, or throw her book on the floor, or declare she never could learn. But now she has left off crying when she is hurt, and tries to bear the pain quietly. When she is sick she does not fret or complain, but takes her medicine without a word. When she is sewing she does not twitch her thread into knots, and when she is writing she writes slowly and carefully. I have rocked her to sleep a thousand times. I have been shut up in the closet with her again and again. And I hope I have done her some good, and taught her some useful lessons."

"Indeed you have, Aunt Patience!" said Susy's papa. "But Susy is not yet perfect. We shall need you six years longer."

And now the little angel Faith opened his golden book, and began to read.

"I have taught Susy that there is another world besides this, and have told her that is her real home, and what a beautiful and happy one it is. I have told her a great deal about Jesus, and the holy angels. I do not know much myself. I am not very old. But if I stay here six years longer, I shall grow wiser, and I will teach Susy all I learn, and we will pray together every morning and every night, till at last she loves the Lord Jesus with all her heart and soul, and mind and strength."

Then Susy's papa and mamma looked at each other and smiled, and they both said: "O beautiful Angel! never leave her!" and the angel answered: "I will stay with her as long as she lives, and will never leave her till I leave her at the very door of Heaven!"

Then the teachers began to put up their books, and Susy's papa and mamma kissed her and said: "We have had a great deal of comfort in our little daughter. And with God's blessing, we shall see her grow up a loving, patient, and obedient child; full of joy and peace, and rich in faith and good works!" So they all bade each other good-night, and went thankfully to bed.

CPSIA information can be obtained
at www.ICGtesting.com
Printed in the USA
LVHW101348160422
716387LV00003B/229

9 783752 594218